D1608411

Julie the Rockhound

By Gail Langer Karwoski   Illustrated by Lisa Downey

Julie saw something sparkle on the hillside behind her new house. She picked up a rock as big as her thumb. The rock had shiny, flat sides and a pointy end. It was beautiful!

She ran down the hill to show it to her dad. They washed it off, and he called it a crystal.

"Like the crystal bowl that Mom keeps on the dining room table?" Julie asked.

Dad shook his head and smiled. "You found a crystal, Julie. But it's not the same as the crystal in the bowl. You found quartz."

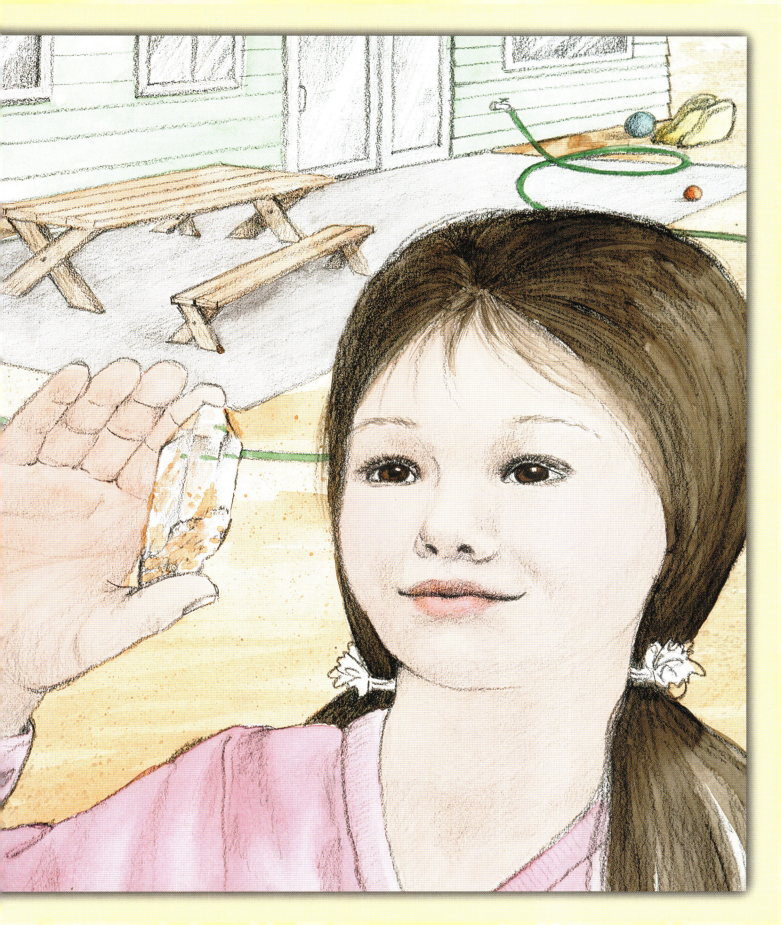

Julie was puzzled. "Like quarts of milk?"

"Quartz sounds like the word for quarts of milk or juice," Dad explained. "But your crystal is made of quartz; a mineral spelled with a "tz." Quartz comes from a vein."

Now Julie was really confused. She traced the light blue vein that carried blood to her hand. "Like the vein in my arm?"

Dad laughed. "Your crystal comes from a vein in the ground where liquid rock used to flow, sort of like a vein that carries blood inside a body."

Julie showed her dad where she found her crystal. She helped him dig a deep, wide hole. In the hole, they found many sparkly crystals poking into a small cavity.

"Look! Here's a pocket of crystals," Dad said.

Grinning, Julie slipped her hand into her pocket. "I know," she said, "but not the same as a pocket in clothes!"

Julie washed and sorted the crystals. Some were clear as window panes. Others were white as clouds.

"Quartz comes in other colors, too," Dad said. He showed Julie a page in his book of minerals. "When quartz is brown or grey, it's called smoky quartz. When it's pink, it's called rose quartz. Purple quartz is amethyst. Yellow is citrine.

Julie looked disappointed. "So my crystal is not special?"

"Your crystal is special because you found it yourself and because it's clear," Dad said.

"Most quartz is only white chunks."

Clear Quartz

Amethyst

White Quartz

Smoky Quartz

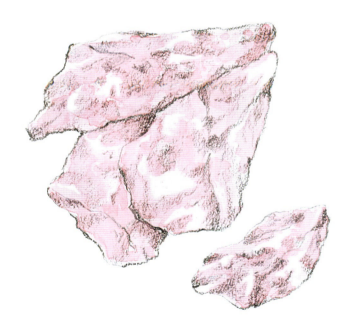

Rose Quartz

Citrine

Dad held up Julie's crystal, and she could see the green of the treetops through it.

He placed it on top of a word in his book, and Julie saw three reflections of that word.

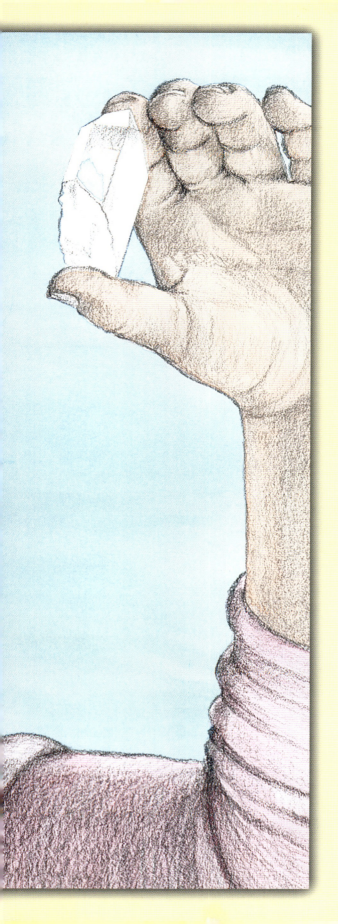

"Are my crystal's flat sides where it got broken?" Julie asked.

"No, those are the crystal's faces."

Julie giggled. "I know! They're not the same as people's faces!"

She counted the faces on each of the quartz crystals. Even though some of the crystals were longer or wider, each had six sides and a pointy end. "All these crystals have the same shape," she said.

"That's because they're all made of the same material: silicon dioxide."

"Silly what?"

"Silicon dioxide. That's the same chemical that makes up glass. Sometimes silicon dioxide gets dissolved in water. If conditions are just right, it grows into crystals."

"Crystals grow?" Julie asked.

"Yes, crystals grow," Dad said. "It takes a VERY long time though. The longer the crystals have to grow, the longer, wider, and heavier they become.

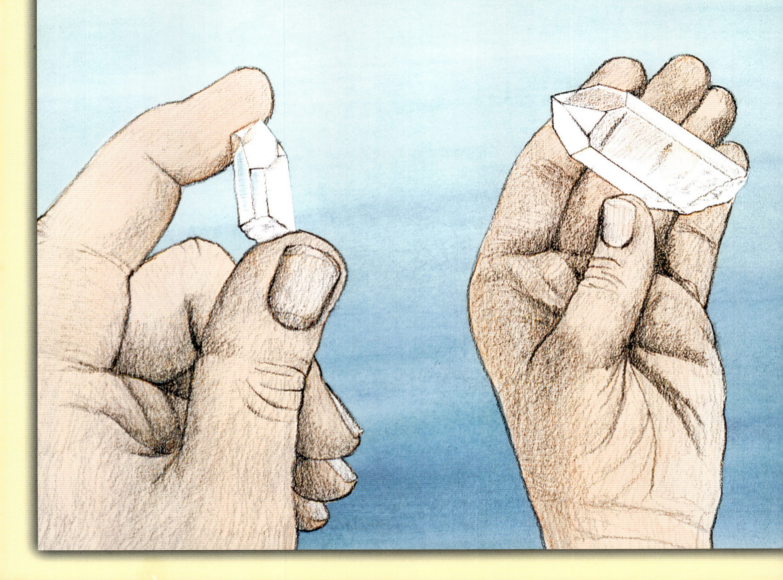

"That's like people!" Julie said. We grow longer and wider and heavier. But we always keep the same basic shape.

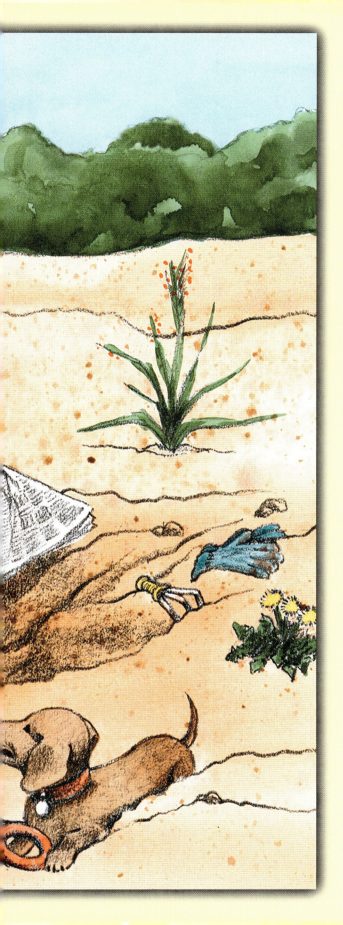

The afternoon sun beat down on the hillside. "I'm tired," Julie complained. "I'm hot. Can we go home now?"

Dad began to pack their quartz crystals into a box. "You have to be patient if you want to be a rockhound," he said.

"What's a rockhound?" Julie asked.

"Hounds follow trails and dig," Dad said. "When you search for sparkly rocks and dig them up, you are like a hound.

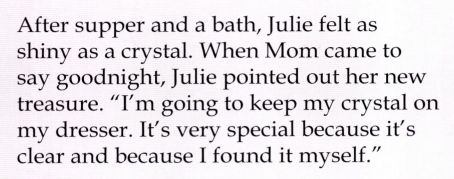

After supper and a bath, Julie felt as shiny as a crystal. When Mom came to say goodnight, Julie pointed out her new treasure. "I'm going to keep my crystal on my dresser. It's very special because it's clear and because I found it myself."

Then she howled like a puppy. "Call me Julie the Rockhound!"

For Creative Minds

For easy use, the "For Creative Minds" educational section may be photocopied or downloaded from www.SylvanDellPublishing.com by the owner of this book. Please do not write in the book.

You may not have seen a quartz crystal like the one that Julie found in this story, but you've probably seen quartz. Tan beach sand is mostly quartz that has weathered into tiny bits.

Quartz is one of the most common minerals on earth. A mineral is a natural solid that has its own chemical makeup and crystal structure. Minerals are the "building blocks" of our world. They can be metal ores like silver and gold, or they can be crystals like the quartz that Julie found. The salt you put on your food is a mineral too.

Plant, animal, or mineral? A matching activity

Minerals are combined together to make different things, both in nature (rocks) and by humans. Which of these things come from or are made from plants, animals, or minerals?

steak

chalk

tan beach sand

eggs

salad

cotton t-shirt

orange juice

wool sweater

jewelry

Plants: salad, orange juice, cotton t-shirt
Animals: steak, egg, wool sweater
Minerals: chalk, tan beach sand, jewelry

Become a rockhound!

Searching for rocks and minerals can be lots of fun. However, you should get permission from the person who owns the land where you will be searching. It's very unusual to find a quartz crystal sticking up out of the ground. You won't find them in grassy areas. Like Julie, you might find them in rocky areas that have been disturbed.

Where:

- at construction sites where there has been digging (get permission and be careful)
- in dried-up river or creek beds
- in woods or areas where tree roots have pushed rocks out of the ground
- on rocky cliff sides (with an adult)

Make sure that you are dressed properly:

- old jeans or long, sturdy pants that can get dirty or stained
- heavy shoes or sneakers—no sandals or flip-flops
- sun hat and sunscreen if you are out in a sunny area
- leather or heavy garden gloves
- a hard hat if you are digging out of a wall or cliff above your head
- safety glasses if you are using a hammer or chisel

Basic tools (depending on where you are digging):

- garden claw
- shovel or trowel
- chisel, rock hammer, or sledgehammer

Other items you might want to have with you:

- lots of water and some snacks
- bug spray
- first aid kit
- cushion to sit or kneel on
- plastic sandwich bags or heavy paper to wrap rocks
- marker to identify where you found each rock
- magnifying glass to study your rocks and minerals

Once you have decided where you will dig for rocks, determine which tools you'll need. If you are digging in the ground, you might want to use a trowel, shovel, or garden claw. If you are digging in a rocky area, you may need a rock hammer or sledgehammer, but only use these with an adult's help.

When you find a neat looking rock or mineral, dig around it to get it out.

Wrap or place it in a plastic bag and identify where you found it and the date. That will help you with your collection later on.

Rocks and minerals found outdoors will probably be covered with clay and dirt; you can wash them with an old toothbrush. If there is a lot of clay, try leaving them outside for a few days. Once the clay has dried, it should be easier to wash off.

Use a guide to help you identify your crystals or rocks, and make labels. You have started a rock collection!

Rocks and how they are formed

ALL rocks are made of minerals; it just depends on how they are put together. There are **THREE** types of rocks, each made a little differently:

Sedimentary Rocks: Sediments are particles such as sand, mud, minerals, shells or even pieces of decaying matter from plants or animals. Sediment builds up over the years, like on a beach. Over a long time, the pressure of all the layers presses the sediment into rock. Limestone, sandstone, and shale are all sedimentary rocks. Cement is a man-made sedimentary rock.

Igneous Rocks: These rocks are made from hot, liquid rock (called "magma" when it is below the earth's surface and "lava" when it is above the surface) that has cooled into a solid. If igneous rock is formed from magma below the earth's surface, then it cools into a rock with grains/minerals you can see (like the granite in countertops). If the hot, liquid rock reached the earth's surface through a volcanic eruption, then the lava cools into volcanic glass (obsidian), or rocks with lots and lots of holes (like pumice).

Metamorphic Rocks: Heat and/or pressure can change sedimentary or igneous rocks into a new type of rock: metamorphic. The word metamorphic means "to change." Limestone, for example, can be changed into marble by pressure.

Food Rocks!

The recipes below may serve as models to understand how rocks are formed.

Sedimentary Rocks: Take one slice of white bread and one slice of wheat/rye bread and remove the crusts. Spread a layer of margarine on the top side of one slice of bread. Make a sandwich by adding a slice of yellow cheese and a slice of ham or turkey as the filling. Pretend that each of these layers is made of particles like some of the sediments we talked about earlier. Can you see the layers you might see in a sedimentary rock? Some are very thin (like the margarine), some are medium (like the meat & cheese), and some are thicker (like the bread).

Given the right circumstances, any kind of rock can be changed to another. Now we can model changing a sedimentary rock to a metamorphic one by adding heat and pressure (remember the word METAMORPHIC means CHANGED!).

Metamorphic Rocks: Get an adult to help you with the waffle iron or the stove! Put your "sedimentary sandwich" onto a hot waffle iron or flat frying pan. Close the sides of the waffle/sandwich iron or press down with a spatula to apply both heat and pressure. After a minute or two, take out your grilled cheese sandwich. How have the layers changed? Like a metamorphic rock, it was changed by heat and pressure into a (delicious) new form.

Igneous Rocks: With an adult's help, melt chocolate chips over a double boiler. Place a cookie pan on a table, but lean one end of the pan on a stack of napkins to create a tilt. Pretend the heated chocolate is lava and pour some onto the sheet pan. Watch it flow down the surface, just as though it had poured out of the top of the volcano. Can you see how it cools and hardens quickly? This is how some igneous rocks form. Now turn off the burner and allow the rest of the chocolate "magma" in the pot to cool. Because it is such a thick layer, it will harden and cool more slowly. This is how some igneous rocks (like the granite in countertops) form.

Sorting it all out – classifying minerals

Geologists do some basic tests when they want to identify minerals in the field. These tests help scientists compare some of the minerals' physical properties. Scientists will look at the color, the shape of the crystal, the luster (if it is shiny or dull), whether the mineral leaves a streak, and how hard it is. Even if you have different samples, the same mineral will show the same properties. No one individual property is enough to identify a mineral.

One of the best tests is for hardness. On a scale of one to ten (Moh's Hardness Scale) the harder the mineral is, the higher the number. If a mineral scratches another mineral, it is harder than the one it scratched.

See if you can match the mineral to its number on the Moh's Hardness Scale. Tools that geologist use to test the hardness of the minerals are given. Put the minerals in order from softest to hardest using the scale below:

> - A **diamond** scratches everything
> - **Quartz** **scratches steel**
> - **Topaz** scratches **quartz**
> - A **sapphire** (corundum) scratches **topaz**
> - Everything scratches **talc**

Moh's Hardness Scale

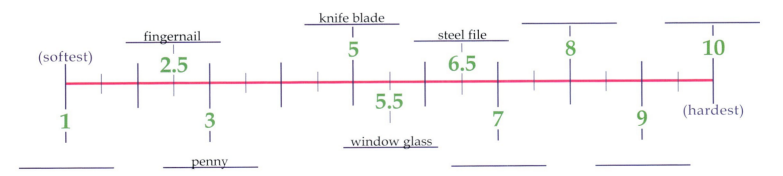

Answers: 1-talc, 7-quartz, 8-topaz, 9-sapphire, 10-diamond

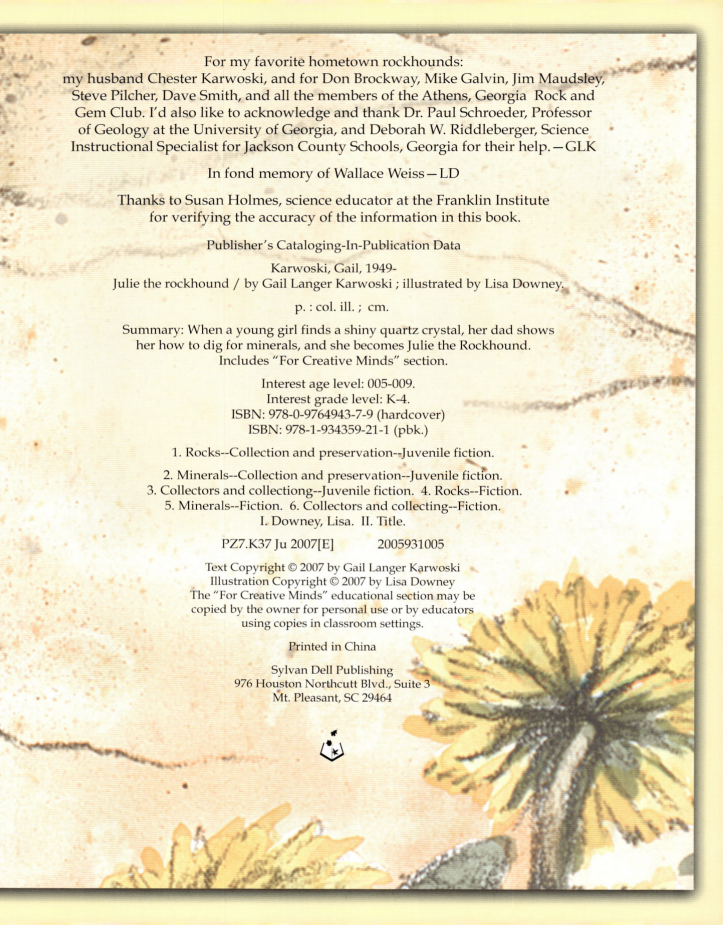

For my favorite hometown rockhounds:
my husband Chester Karwoski, and for Don Brockway, Mike Galvin, Jim Maudsley,
Steve Pilcher, Dave Smith, and all the members of the Athens, Georgia Rock and
Gem Club. I'd also like to acknowledge and thank Dr. Paul Schroeder, Professor
of Geology at the University of Georgia, and Deborah W. Riddleberger, Science
Instructional Specialist for Jackson County Schools, Georgia for their help. —GLK

In fond memory of Wallace Weiss—LD

Thanks to Susan Holmes, science educator at the Franklin Institute
for verifying the accuracy of the information in this book.

Publisher's Cataloging-In-Publication Data

Karwoski, Gail, 1949-
Julie the rockhound / by Gail Langer Karwoski ; illustrated by Lisa Downey.

p. : col. ill. ; cm.

Summary: When a young girl finds a shiny quartz crystal, her dad shows
her how to dig for minerals, and she becomes Julie the Rockhound.
Includes "For Creative Minds" section.

Interest age level: 005-009.
Interest grade level: K-4.
ISBN: 978-0-9764943-7-9 (hardcover)
ISBN: 978-1-934359-21-1 (pbk.)

1. Rocks--Collection and preservation--Juvenile fiction.

2. Minerals--Collection and preservation--Juvenile fiction.
3. Collectors and collectiong--Juvenile fiction. 4. Rocks--Fiction.
5. Minerals--Fiction. 6. Collectors and collecting--Fiction.
I. Downey, Lisa. II. Title.

PZ7.K37 Ju 2007[E]   2005931005

Text Copyright © 2007 by Gail Langer Karwoski
Illustration Copyright © 2007 by Lisa Downey
The "For Creative Minds" educational section may be
copied by the owner for personal use or by educators
using copies in classroom settings.

Printed in China

Sylvan Dell Publishing
976 Houston Northcutt Blvd., Suite 3
Mt. Pleasant, SC 29464